The first...of (a) stellar, long-running (military) romantic suspense series.

— *The Night is Mine*, Booklist, "The 20 Best Romantic Suspense Novels: Modern Masterpieces"

I knew the books would be good, but I didn't realize how good.

— Night Stalkers series, Kirkus Reviews

Buchman mixes adrenalin-spiking battles and brusque military jargon with a sensitive approach.

— Publishers Weekly

13 times "Top Pick of the Month"

— Night Owl Reviews

I0533038

PRAISE FOR M. L. BUCHMAN

Tom Clancy fans open to a strong female lead will clamor for more.

— *DRONE*, PUBLISHERS WEEKLY

Superb! Miranda is utterly compelling!

— *BOOKLIST*, STARRED REVIEW

Miranda Chase continues to astound and charm.

— BARB M.

Escape Rating: A. Five Stars! OMG just start with *Drone* and be prepared for a fantastic binge-read!

— READING REALITY

The best military thriller I've read in a very long time. Love the female characters.

— *DRONE*, SHELDON MCARTHUR, FOUNDER OF THE MYSTERY BOOKSTORE, LA

A fabulous soaring thriller.

— *TAKE OVER AT MIDNIGHT*, MIDWEST BOOK REVIEW

Meticulously researched, hard-hitting, and suspenseful.

— *Pure Heat*, Publishers Weekly, starred review

Expert technical details abound, as do realistic military missions with superb imagery that will have readers feeling as if they are right there in the midst and on the edges of their seats.

— *Light Up the Night*, RT Reviews, 4 1/2 stars

Buchman has catapulted his way to the top tier of my favorite authors.

— Fresh Fiction

Nonstop action that will keep readers on the edge of their seats.

— *Take Over at Midnight*, Library Journal

M L. Buchman's ability to keep the reader right in the middle of the action is amazing.

— Long and Short Reviews

The only thing you'll ask yourself is, "When does the next one come out?"

— *Wait Until Midnight*, RT Reviews, 4 stars

SWIFTWATER RESCUE

A MILITARY ROMANTIC SUSPENSE STORY

M. L. BUCHMAN

Buchman Bookworks

Copyright 2020 Matthew Lieber Buchman

All titles were previously published separately by Buchman Bookworks, Inc. All introductions are new to this collection.

All rights reserved.

This book, or parts thereof, may not be reproduced in any form without permission from the author.

Receive a free book and discover more by this author at: www.mlbuchman.com

Cover images:

The source of the Selenginka River from Sobolinoe Lake © avrutin

US Army UH-60 Black Hawk helicopter © Michael Kaplan | Wikimedia

SIGN UP FOR M. L. BUCHMAN'S NEWSLETTER TODAY

and receive:
Release News
Free Short Stories
a Free Book

Get your free book today. Do it now.
free-book.mlbuchman.com

Other works by M. L. Buchman: *(* - also in audio)*

Other works by M. L. Buchman:

Contemporary Romance (cont)

Love Abroad
Heart of the Cotswolds: England
Path of Love: Cinque Terre, Italy

Where Dreams
Where Dreams are Born
Where Dreams Reside
Where Dreams Are of Christmas*
Where Dreams Unfold
Where Dreams Are Written

Science Fiction / Fantasy

Deities Anonymous
Cookbook from Hell: Reheated
Saviors 101

Single Titles
The Nara Reaction
Monk's Maze
the Me and Elsie Chronicles

Non-Fiction

Strategies for Success
Managing Your Inner Artist/Writer
Estate Planning for Authors*
Character Voice
Narrate and Record Your Own
Audiobook*

Short Story Series by M. L. Buchman:

Romantic Suspense

Delta Force
Th Delta Force Shooters
The Delta Force Warriors

Firehawks
The Firehawks Lookouts
The Firehawks Hotshots
The Firebirds

The Night Stalkers
The Night Stalkers 5D Stories
The Night Stalkers 5E Stories
The Night Stalkers CSAR
The Night Stalkers Wedding Stories

US Coast Guard

White House Protection Force

Contemporary Romance

Eagle Cove

Henderson's Ranch*

Where Dreams

Action-Adventure Thrillers

Dead Chef

Miranda Chase Origin Stories

Science Fiction / Fantasy

Deities Anonymous

Other
The Future Night Stalkers
Single Titles

ABOUT THIS TITLE

Combat Medic Allyson Hanover must face the impossible, the loss of two lives that were in her hands — before a raging Colombian river ripped them away.

When fellow *Medic Reuben Fehlman* joins a field test to develop new swiftwater rescue techniques, they both land in the rushing waters on Henderson's Ranch. Emily, Mark, Michael, and even Noreen can't crack it.

To survive the swiftwater? The two of them must brave the current — together.

PROLOGUE

Medic of the bird.

Sergeant Allyson J. Hanover cursed because that wasn't going to be enough this time. Of course, she gave that curse every time the US Army's 160th Night Stalkers were called in. Others said she was nuts, but the mindset worked for her: this time she'd do better than *every* time before.

Tonight's skirmish, with a supposedly small and isolated cocaine lab along the Río Samaná, had flashed into a hard battle against horrendous odds. The heart of the Colombian jungle was ablaze with gunfire.

Her MH-60M Black Hawk helicopter had been hanging back from the battle. Combat search and rescue was hard on some people. Pilots wanted to be in the fray. Crew chiefs itched to unleash their Miniguns.

Death waits in the dark, one of the Night Stalkers' mottos, had a different meaning for medics than it did for the flight crews.

Christian, Jewish, or even staunch atheist, all medics prayed for boredom.

Not tonight.

A radio call crackled in from the battle to their east, almost unintelligible through the background gunfire.

"Two fallen off the bridge—" grand phrase for the rickety foot bridge that had become the center of the battle "—and now in the water. Heading west with the current. Condition unknown." The worst phrase in the world to Allyson's ears.

"Wounded" meant that someone was nearby enough to be tending them.

"Dead" meant there was no rush beyond securing the body before the bad guys did.

"Condition unknown" meant that every passing second could be one second too many.

The Black Hawk nosed down sharply enough that Allyson had to grab hold of her strapped-down "heavy" medic bag to avoid sliding forward. Every medic had a different setup—most combined into a single bag. She preferred two: "light" and "heavy." The light bag covered everything she'd usually need. Heavy bag (which actually weighed less) covered trauma kits, chest crackers, and all of the other nasties that only a CSAR medic could need without being a licensed surgeon.

As the helo's twin turbines climbed up from dull roar to angry shriek, they dove down into the canyon. The Río Samaná Norte had joined the main river twenty kilometers east of here, in the heart of the Cordillera Oriental mountains. Below them it rushed through the jungle, plummeting over the hard rapids and abrupt waterfalls of the steep descent toward the Río Magdalena valley.

"Dicey," Captain Berman called back over the intercom.

Allyson snapped on her three-meter Monkey Tail safety line, tugged to make sure it was anchored to both her vest and the overhead D-ring. Then she opened the side cargo door, made sure it latched so that it wouldn't try to guillotine her, and leaned out into the wind to study the river.

The Samaná was wide enough here that the trees couldn't span the width between the banks—quite. Sixty-five feet of Black Hawk could descend all the way down to the water in precious few places.

They continued tracing the winding water upriver toward the battle.

Just as her usual, we'll-never-find-them nerves were kicking in, she spotted the bright flash in her night-vision gear.

"Infrared flash. Three hundred meters upriver. Moving fast toward us." Good news: the soldier had been undamaged enough to activate his emergency infrared locator. Bad news: the river was fast and rough here.

"Roger. In sight."

Berman sent them through a gut-wrenching twist.

To the only open patch for a long distance into the dark.

A brief widening in the river.

Only one chance.

Beyond that was a major rapids and a waterfall that unloaded onto boulders, not some deep pool.

She ignored the chatter on the intercom and did her best to keep the infrared flasher in sight.

Crew Chief Thompson came up beside her, with a winch cable in his hand.

He double-checked her Monkey Tail. She did the same for him. Now, if either of them fell, it would be under three meters. From the top of the cargo deck, they'd be stopped barely a meter past the open door.

Together, they leaned out of the helo as it settled sideways with its wheels in the water. The other crew chief was firing short bursts from his Minigun upriver as targets presented themselves.

Both she and Thompson prepared for the grab as Berman kept the wide cargo door facing toward the current, the deck mere inches above the tumbling water. As the water splashed and twisted, the occasional stream flowed through the cargo deck and out the other side door. Bathtub warm, it flowed through, rich with the scents of the dense jungle—mostly rotting biomass.

Thompson was reading out the current and Unknown Condition's course as he was washed toward them. The pilot would be concentrating on too many other factors to watch the vagaries of the victim's passage.

"Back five feet. Forward two." Unknown swept around the wrong side of a large boulder. "Back seven. Two more."

"Hold!"

They both leaned out to grab the face-down soldier—bad sign.

Even as she managed to grab the shoulder of his vest, she could feel it was mistake.

The soldier rolled face-up in her grasp, Thompson managed to snap the winch hook onto the D-ring at the center of the soldier's chest.

Did he sputter? Still alive?

But, even secured, he was dragged beneath the helo.

Allyson was almost dragged out as well before she lost her grip.

The spooled-out length of winch cable was too long to keep him above the surface.

Before she could yell out for Berman to climb, a second body slammed into the edge of the cargo deck.

No flasher.

Immersed in the warm water there was minimal

infrared signature in her night-vision goggles. She needed a good ten degrees of difference to see a body clearly.

She hadn't seen him coming.

This one was definitely alive. He managed to hook his elbows over the edge of the deck.

Allyson grabbed one arm to keep him there. Then reached out for the more secure handhold of his vest to haul him aboard. No vest. That meant—

With his free hand, the swimmer jammed a large knife upward under Thompson's chin.

Time slowed.

She could see the assailant twist the knife for maximum damage. But, when he tried to yank it free to attack her, it stuck.

The chief collapsed sideways onto Allyson, slamming her hard against the door jamb.

Her head rang despite the helmet.

Then, the current won, and dragged the attacker from her grasp and under the helicopter.

He, too, was gone.

By the time she could call out for Berman to lift clear, she knew it was too little too late.

Thompson lay dead on the cargo deck, the blade still plunged in his throat to the hilt.

A lifeless body dangled from the winch cable.

Tonight, she hadn't been good enough.

1

———

"Major Lang. A moment please, ma'am."

Allyson had struggled with this for days. And now that it was basically too late, they were less than a fifty meters from the helicopters waiting to take them aloft.

Stupid time to ask...she glanced around at the busy traffic of Gray's Airfield at Joint Base Lewis-McChord. The Night Stalkers, returning from training flights, were settling into their slots. The regular Army were just heading aloft for theirs.

And their two helos were waiting for them.

The major turned slowly to look at her.

Allyson bit her lower lip, but it she knew she was going to ask anyway.

That Major Lois Lang was a bit terrifying was a lousy excuse for delaying so long, but it was all that Allyson had at the moment.

She knew a number of pilots, Night Stalkers pilots, who had failed to meet the major's requirements for CSAR. There was some crucial test that no one ever talked about beyond its name: "The Khyber." Those who passed would only shudder when it was mentioned. Those who failed looked either shell-shocked or ready to puke afterwards.

"The Khyber," one flunked reject had whispered to her before shipping back to the 2nd Battalion, "is worse than the Kobayashi Maru."

It had taken her a while to track down the reference. A Star Trek—what was it with helo pilots and Star Trek?—test of character, a true no-win scenario.

Apparently a nasty one.

"Proceed." Major Lang looked crisp and freshly pressed, carrying a small PG—Personal Gear bag. Allyson felt like a bumbling trainwreck wearing her "heavy" pack, and trying to juggle her own PG, plus her light medic pack.

"These orders, ma'am," Allyson held up the crumpled sheet in her hand that was also holding the PG's handles. The paper snapped and rattled in the chill wind of the October morning. The scudding clouds of the Pacific Northwest looked ready to back it up with a lashing rain in the next few minutes. But this was her last chance, and she had to do it now.

She attempted to hand the sheet over.

"I wrote those. I'm aware of what they say." Though they were the same height, she made Allyson feel small. They both wore the same flight suits, but the Major carried a helmet with a Superman S on the side. Super*woman.*

No way to compete with that.

Her own had the Ancient Greek letters Eta, Mu, Beta—the first letters of the Hippocratic *Epidemics* "Do no harm"—and a small bust of Hippocrates. No one recognized any of it, of course. The few who asked were careful to never bring it up again. Seriously obscure. Especially when compared to the major's "Superwoman" declaration.

And she was.

Below the edge of Major Lang's flight suit, one foot was booted but her mechanical one was there for all to see. No attempt to hide anything. Since losing her foot, she'd remade 5th Battalion Night Stalkers CSAR in her own image. She'd done it so well, that they were now retooling the rest of the regiment to match.

Get your act together, Hanover. "Request to be released from this training."

"Reason?"

Allyson looked at the crumpled-up page as the first few spatters of chilly rain blotched onto the paper. "It's a night I'd rather not relive."

"Were you sleeping with Chief Thompson?"

"What? No! I barely knew him. It's just..." She didn't know what.

"Did you know the soldier who died?"

She just shook her head, knowing her two best outs were gone.

"You know, sergeant, when I lost this..." Major Lang tapped her mechanical foot on the ground. The rubber sole made it sound just like a boot. "...I gave up. A good man taught me a hard lesson about what it really meant to be a Night Stalker."

"Harder than losing your foot and the ability to fly CSAR?"

"Yes."

"Shit! Sorry, ma'am. Must have been a hell of a lesson."

"It was. Would you like to know what he taught me?"

Allyson wasn't sure if she was ready for it, but as the engines on their helicopters were spinning to life, she decided that she couldn't feel much worse.

"Yes, ma'am." Allyson braced herself.

In answer, Major Lois Lang held up her helmet and

turned it so that Allyson could read the four letters across the back.

NSDQ.

Night Stalkers Don't Quit.

The regiment's other motto.

"When you *truly* understand these four letters, Sergeant Hanover, that's when you've done something. Now you can walk on this if you want to. You're one of our best medics, so we won't be remanding you back to regular forces if you do. If that concern is was what made you wait until this late moment to make your request."

Allyson could feel the blood drain out of her face. Lose the Night Stalkers? She hadn't even thought about the possibility. She worked so hard to get here that it was unimaginable. They were the best, and she never wanted to be anywhere else.

"So. Not that." The major smiled to herself for a moment, but Allyson didn't know how to read it. "Okay, Sergeant. Here's the bottom line. Heliborne swiftwater rescue training isn't part of our CSAR training—yet. We're developing something new here, and we're doing it specifically because of your mission's...challenges in Colombia last month. Your insights could be uniquely valuable, but I'll understand if you want to walk away." She may have phrased it as if Allyson had a choice, but did she?

It was *her* anchoring the drug-lab's enforcer on the cargo deck that had provided the leverage for him to kill Crew Chief Thompson. She owed the crew chief for that. But more so, she owed the first soldier. Had he sputtered with life, before her attempt to save him drowned him instead? She'd never know, yet it had haunted her dreams every night since.

The major didn't say anything else.

Allyson stared at the helmet. It was one of the things she'd loved most about the Night Stalkers.

NSDQ.

Her own family's motto? *Whatever.*

No tradition of New England "can do" attitude. No hardy Western "get her done" ethos. Her family—Pennsylvania mill town trailer trash. Laid off? Food stamps and welfare were just fine. Found some work? Sure...whatever.

"Thank you for your time, Major."

Major Lois Lang nodded, donned her helmet, and turned for the helo.

Allyson studied her own helmet. Eta Mu Beta. Do no harm.

Yeah, right up there with... Allyson sighed, ...Lambda Beta Sigma, *Latre, therapeuson seauton*—Physician, heal thyself.

Crap!

Allyson jammed the orders into her PG bag and followed the major.

2

"READY FOR SOME FUN?"

"Uh, sure." Allyson looked at the woman waiting in the back of the Black Hawk. The first thing she'd noticed was the big medic bag. The new medic was a one-bagger—already hung on the rear cargo net. No, she also had a tiny backpack with a medic's cross close to hand. Allyson hung her two bags beside the big one.

"You find the small field pack useful?" Allyson asked the medic.

"Hell, yeah! When I have to get off the helo, it covers the very worst. But, Holy Crap, you're ready a whole war by yourself, Hippocrates."

Allyson twisted around to look at her. It took another medic to recognize the face on her helmet. Maybe she recognized the Ancient Greek acronym as well? No, it was better not to ask. Because then she'd have to explain, and that never went well.

As the crew chief slammed the big cargo door shut, the Black Hawk lifted. Out the window she could see the big, twin-rotor Chinook climbing aloft as well. It seemed odd to bring the big cargo helo on a CSAR training exercise, but Major Lang must have her reasons.

"Noreen Wallace from Muskogee, Oklahoma," the medic's handshake was strong, and it was impossible to not feel cheered by it. She was also runway beautiful.

That's when Allyson noted that, in addition to the sword-and-twined-snakes of a medic patch on her sleeve, she also wore captain's bars.

Allyson saluted sharply.

"Yeah, I know," Noreen returned it casually. "Went ROTC pre-med, but I love being a medic too much to get out of the back of a helo. That's Xavier," she nodded toward the right-side crew chief.

"Hey there, ma'am." He was a massive man with skin even darker than Noreen's. "Guess I'm from Muskogee now, too."

"Damn straight," Noreen shot back at him. They were a couple? And serving together? That was seriously strange.

Noreen...Wallace?

Major Lang had called Allyson *one of CSAR's top medics.*

There wasn't really competition between medics but at the singular Night Stalker "top medic" pinnacle there was just one name, Noreen Wallace.

"Staff Sergeant Allyson Hanover, from..." nowhere she wanted to admit to, "...Joint Base Lewis-McChord."

"Sounds like both Xavier and my sister-in-law. No home but the Army until she married my big brother. They were both backenders, too, just like Xavier."

"Shit, woman! Comparing me to the two top mechanics in the Night Stalkers is plain cruel."

"It's a compliment," Noreen's wink said that was just the reaction she'd expected.

Top medic. Top two mechanics. A whole family of

serious overachievers. Would have been nice to grow up knowing that was even possible.

"That's probably why I stick here every time they try to bump me into officer country or off to med school, though Mama would love having a doctor in family. 'We Wallace's are really in it now,' she'd say with one of her big laughs. Except for my brother and me our family is just a happy bunch of Okie farmers. Your parents die in the military like Connie's? Sorry, I'm nosy as hell. Feel free to tell me to shut up. I won't, but it doesn't bother me a bit when you try to stop me."

Xavier's eye roll confirmed that reality.

"Uh, no. They're alive. They're just…" Allyson tried a deep breath and felt even more jittery. "They wouldn't understand."

"A misfit, huh? Cool. I like that. You got someone?"

Allyson decided that double-checking her gear was the only safe answer.

"Ooo!" Noreen made an excited noise.

"Hush, woman," Xavier's deep voice sounded amused at his wife's answering growl, but she didn't push.

Allyson welcomed the chance to try and catch up with herself.

Her med gear was finally set just the way she liked it during a transit. She could pull two zippers, dropping open the big front flaps, and she'd be in rescue configuration with everything precisely where she needed it.

Out the window, they were climbing above the unsettled weather. One nice thing about Western Washington, the weather might come in thick, but it wasn't often very deep. They were soon up at fifteen thousand feet, riding in the sun. The occasional peak stuck its snow-and-rock summit up through the clouds like fir-covered islands punching up out of Puget Sound beneath the cloud cover, but mostly it was the peaceful world of fluffy white and shining blue.

As she tucked her personal bag behind the rear net, she remembered her orders. She pulled them out and decrinkled them as well as she could.

Staff Sergeant Allyson J. Hanover

160th Special Operations Aviation Regiment, 5th Battalion, D Company

Five-day training course development: Swiftwater Rescue

Henderson's Ranch, Montana

"You ever heard of this place?" she asked Noreen. It didn't really matter, she'd find out soon enough, but it seemed a subtle way to apologize for cutting Noreen off earlier.

Noreen pumped her fist and began chanting, "Emily! Emily! Em-i-ly!"

As if that told Allyson anything.

3

HENDERSON'S RANCH WAS TWENTY THOUSAND ACRES OF horse ranch tucked up against the foothills of the Rockies.

An overnight dusting of snow and browned grass crunched beneath Allyson's feet as she disembarked, but the sun felt warm on her face. She zipped up her jacket quickly and fished out a pair of gloves.

When the rotor blades swung to a halt after a final lazy *whoop-whoop,* her ears rang with the vastness of the silence. Her world was never this quiet. If the bustle of one of America's largest military bases ever flagged for a moment, I-5 ran close beside JBLM. In Colombia, she'd been based off the USS *Peleliu,* and the old helicopter carrier was never silent.

Here, the silence was so deep that her ears rang.

The landscape was stark as well. Instead of the thickly overwhelming Douglas fir forest of the Pacific Northwest, or the teeming biomass of the Colombian jungle, the few trees here were gathered in small copses of larch and pine. Each smell was sharp and distinct on the air: horse, grass, pine... and snow. She could actually smell the snow.

A couple strolled out from the sprawling two-story ranch house to meet them.

"Major Lang and her gang," the big, broad-shouldered man offered a saucy salute. His jet-black hair brushed his collar, but his eye color was hidden behind mirrored shades. He hadn't bothered to don more than a flannel shirt against the chill slicing past Allyson's blood, thinned by four months of anti-drug interdiction missions in the tropics.

Major Lang returned it much more casually than was her norm. "Major Henderson. Major Beale."

"Hi Lois, I'm retired. It's Emily and you know it." The lovely blonde answered but returned the salute. She at least had pulled on a denim jacket with a wool lining, though she hadn't bothered to zip it up.

That's when the names registered. Majors Henderson and Beale, the famous founders of the 5th Battalion D Company. Her unit. She'd joined after they were gone, and had never got to meet them. But here they were.

Henderson's Ranch. She should have known, somehow, when she saw the name. Noreen's chant of "Emily!" made more sense now.

Their pilot sauntered around the nose of the Black Hawk. Of course, Major Lola Maloney never walked in any other way that Allyson had seen.

"Hey, you two." Instead of a salute, she offered a friendly slouch and an electric smile.

"Hey, yourself," Mark growled happily at her. "How's the girls?"

"The twins have Tim home for the whole week. Makes all three of them goofy happy." She shuddered. "Only way I could get them all out of my hair for a few days. What the hell, Emily? How did women like us end up being moms? It's just crazy. Lois here offered to fill in as copilot, since this is her gig anyway. Glad to have some women to fly with for a bit."

"That be includin' the likes o' me?" The Chinook pilot came over with his crew which included another medic. It wasn't common to have three CSAR medics all in the same place. Major Lang was taking this swiftwater training even more seriously than Allyson had first thought.

Allyson hadn't met Captain Roberts before, but she'd seen him around—it was hard *not* to notice him. Tall, blond, a thick Texas accent, and a white cowboy hat, that actually *didn't* look ridiculous on him. He and his crew had a fierce reputation in the field; Lang was pulling out all the stops.

"You don't count, Roberts, not even in a pink tutu. Seriously Emily. I actually bought two pink tutus last week. That's just so wrong." Lola was emphatic before she turned back to Roberts. "Besides, you didn't bring your wife along, so we're going to be ignoring you completely. Hey, Carmen," she acknowledged the only woman in the Chinook's crew. She was a short fiery redhead with close-cropped hair, and a flamenco dancer on the helmet that dangled from her fingertips.

"Hey. You got any hot men around here or did you leave them all home?" She looked right past every male in the group, including the Texan, until she focused on the Chinook's copilot. She shouted out, "There's one! He's mine!" and threw herself at him. A less solid man would have gone to the ground. Instead, he caught her easily and kissed her deeply.

"Those two ever going to stop acting like newlyweds?"

"Nope!" Captain Roberts shook his head. "Makes me a tad sorry that my lady is back in Brooklyn."

"Everything okay there?"

"Sure. Her dad's retiring from the police force after forty-seven years."

Lola shoved him hard enough to slam into the side of the Black Hawk. "Why aren't you there, asshole?"

"Hey. I sent him a puppy. Give him something to do with his time."

"What breed?"

"Aussie shepherd mutt."

"You're cruel."

"Man needs something to keep him movin' about some. Figure one of those should do the job just fine."

As if in answer, a pure black Malinois came bounding toward them from the direction of the barn. It made a show of greeting everyone, looked around in surprise, then bolted back to the barn just in time for a trio of women to come trotting out the big door on horses.

"There's your advance team," Emily nodded.

The three women waved as they turned their horses west, and broke into a quick trot with the dog running ahead on point. All three had hair down past their shoulders: dark brunette, auburn red, and a shining white gold. Like they were samples on one of those perfect hair color charts. Her own streaky dishwater blonde wouldn't fit in at all.

"Jodi must be busy with the dogs," Mark raised his voice, but didn't bother looking around at the woman coming up behind him with another Malinois trotting silently at her side. Somehow he'd heard them coming and she hadn't...

Mark was looking over Allyson's own shoulder. She turned around and saw her own shadowed reflection of the glass of the Black Hawk's windshield. The angles were right. When she turned back, Mark was smiling at her. She'd bet there was a wink behind those mirrored shades to go with the grin.

"Nah," the woman who must be Jodi shoved him aside so that she could stand beside Emily. "Brandy's feeling the cold in her hip, she is eleven after all. I didn't want to push her. Hello, everyone. When you're ready to try incorporating dogs in your scenarios, Stan and I have a pair that I think would really suit your needs."

"Dogs?" Major Lang actually looked a little off balance which made Allyson feel better about her own skyrocketing level of anxiety. All this because she'd— Allyson shook her head to clear it. Way too much pressure, even for a Night Stalker.

Jodi scratched the Malinois' head. "You'll see. We have a Spec Ops dog school here. I've been reading up on it and I have a pair of animals I'd like to test in swiftwater rescue scenarios. Brandy and I did a couple of CSAR events when we were out with the SEALs, but all on dry land. We never did swiftwater, did we girl?" The last was in that squeaky high voice all dog handlers used. It sounded ridiculous, but the dog's tail thumped loudly on the dirt in delight. A female SEAL war dog handler?

"Okay," Allyson decided she needed to get control of something in her life. "Is there anything you folks don't do here?"

Emily, Mark, and Jodi all looked at each other, then shrugged in unison.

"Y'all find somethin', you jes let us'n know," Mark spoke in a thick Texas drawl so bad it made Major Roberts snort in laughter.

Jodi rolled her eyes.

Emily just sighed.

4

REUBEN FEHLMAN'S MORNING HAD STARTED JUST LIKE ARMY mornings always seemed to.

Two days ago, he'd been doing a training exercise with the 3rd Battalion of the 160th Night Stalkers regiment in Japan.

Yesterday, he'd been assigned to the 5th, and spent most of it in the air getting to JBLM. So, his body clock was screwed eight ways to Hanukkah.

This morning, there'd been a horrendous pounding on his billet's door.

By his watch he'd either been asleep for an hour or thirteen, and it definitely felt like the former. If it was even on the right time zone.

When he'd creaked the door open, a cute redhead in a flightsuit had been leaning on his doorjamb.

"Cap'n says you're our new medic."

"Oh," had been the brilliant extent of his answer.

She looked him up and down once, then her grin went sideways.

Reuben looked down himself. Jockey shorts.

"Bitchin' outfit. Might be a little cold in the snow though." She snapped her fingers in front of his nose a couple times, close enough to make him blink furiously. "Grab your gear and let's go. Whether or not you get dressed is up to you."

He'd chosen to get dressed.

Following Carmen to a Chinook helicopter, he'd stretched out on the hard deck, rested his head on his medic's bag, and woken three hours later on a Montana horse ranch. Typical Army—no idea what was going on, just show up.

Special Operations Forces had very few women. There were two female pilots and three crew chiefs in all of the 160th's 3rd battalion as far as he knew. Here they were everywhere. It was definitely weird, and he knew absolutely nobody.

He needed a roadmap or he'd be as lost here as Moses had been—wandering the Sinai desert for forty years, and earning himself history's "The Worst Navigator Ever" award hands-down. Reuben had been there. The place just wasn't that damn big.

There were two other medics, which seemed a good place to start. One, a lovely black woman, was chatting with the ranch owners about all sorts of people who didn't appear to be here.

The other medic stood off to the side, looking as uncertain as he felt. He noted the ponytail banner of streaky dark blonde and used it as a guidepost. More people drifted over from different parts of the ranch, but by circling around the back of the Black Hawk, he managed to come up beside her.

"Hi."

"Hi." Her gaze stayed on the rest of the crowd.

"Any idea what's happening?"

"Not a fucking clue," she turned and offered him a reluctant head tip of greeting. "Just know that it's all my fault."

"Good. Now I know who to blame."

She raised a hand, "Got it in one."

He liked the light humor of her tone. Dark, Army humor but, still, it was a relief. "I'll see if I can screw up next. Then Phase II can be on me."

"Don't!" The hint of light that had danced briefly in her amber eyes went dark, and she turned her attention to the dirt. "It's not worth it."

"Shit. Sorry I stepped in it."

She shrugged. "No way to know." Then she glanced briefly at him, and he caught a glimpse of a smile. "But you sure did."

"Fine. Care to tell me medic-to-medic what I stepped in so I don't do a face-plant there myself?" Medic was a whole language unto itself, one that he didn't get to exercise much. Unlike pilots, which came at two per helicopter, medics were often one or two per entire company. The chance to connect and just talk about the job was rare.

Most of the people began drifting toward the big ranch house. She seemed to watch their backs for a moment, before turning and walking in the other direction.

The third medic had disappeared into the depths of the crowd, her position marked only by the towering black man who seemed to be sticking close by her side. The white cowboy hat was another signpost in the thick and happy chatter. Reuben hadn't even met him, he'd just slept in the back of his helo for three hours.

Unsure which to follow, he decided to accompany the blonde medic away from that reunion-type noise.

The sun had driven back the morning's initial chill, and the sky was a great blue arc overhead. Past the huge red barn and garage with big-truck-sized doors, a footpath wound up a knoll thickly covered with brown prairie grass.

At the top, there was a stout wooden bench anchored on a concrete pad.

"What a place to watch the sunrise." The prairie stretched out forever. He was a New York City boy, so it took him a bit to understand the perspective. The odd brown-and-white splotches in the distance weren't some sort of giant flower waving in the wind, they were cattle grazing on the prairie.

Then he spotted two riders on horses wending their way among them. The cattle in perspective were...

"Whoa! Those are seriously big cows."

"Longhorn cattle."

"Oh, how can you tell?"

She pointed down the face of the knoll rather than out toward the range of cattle.

A massive cow stood not fifty feet below them; looking just like every cattle-roundup Western movie he'd ever seen. It tore a clump of grass then raised its head to stare at him.

"Its horns are wider than my *truck*. Do you think he's dangerous?"

There was no sign of any fence between them.

In answer, the cow tore up some more grass.

"I think *she* was wondering the same thing about us, so we should be fine. I'm Allyson by the way."

"Reuben," he sat on the other end of the bench, long enough for two couples. But he kept an eye on the monster cow. "Maybe we should name her Babe, after Paul Bunyan's cow. She's that big."

"But she isn't blue." Allyson delivered the line without even a flicker of a smile.

Then, without any preamble, she told him about her recent mission. Her voice didn't change from medic-analytic for a single moment. Either she was in shock, or she was one seriously chill lady. Not even when she described the stabbing of the crew chief, though he could feel his own throat itch in sympathy.

"It was a perfect thrust: severed brain-stem and shredded hippocampus. I was just lucky that the blade lodged in the throat cartilage or he might have taken a shot at me. So, we're all here because I had a mission go sideways."

"And this Major Lang wants to learn from what happened on your mission."

Allyson shrugged.

"And you think this completely sucks, why?"

"Go away."

"I dunno. It's a pretty comfortable bench with a helluva view."

He didn't look over so she wouldn't take it as a come-on, but he heard her resigned sigh.

"Why does it suck? Because I've already run the scenario a thousand times and I still don't know..." she paused long enough for the giant cow to close its eyes and start a nap, "... what I would have done differently."

"Mighty thoughtful pause there, Medic Allyson."

"Look, they both died on my watch. Can't you just leave it alone?"

"Sounds as if the first one was dead before he even got to you."

Out of the corner of his eye, he saw the flinch. It wasn't

big. She was a trained Special Ops soldier. But so was he, and he saw it.

"You think he wasn't?" Every medic absolutely believed in their ability to save a life, even if the soldier reached them in a condition no ER would even consider wasting time on. It was simply part of the mindset. No prior failure could break that faith for a true medic.

Her shrug said it all. No way to know.

"Aw, shit." He wished he could think of what to do for her.

Out of ideas, he simply sat with her. And watched the giant sleeping cow not named Babe.

5

"You're in."

"You're nuts." Allyson looked down at the water, then up at the retired colonel—somebody Gibson. "This is October, that river is probably glacier fed."

They'd flown out to the edge of the ranch, close by the edge of the Flathead Wilderness. She could see the snow hadn't melted much off these slopes. A noisy waterfall cascaded down from the foothills, splashed into the deep pool swirling in front of them, then the rapids took off for the snowy prairie.

"It is." Then the colonel gave her a sharp push.

She made a grab to take him with her, or maybe spin him around so that he went in and she stayed dry. By the time her fingers closed, he wasn't even there.

Her curse ended with an underwater scream.

It wasn't cold.

It was so astonishingly, unimaginably frigid that every muscle locked up *hard* in one gigantic spasm.

Somehow, she lunged back up into the air. Four feet deep.

Just in time for a flailing Reuben to slam into her and drive them both back into the water.

"No! Wait! Goddamn it, Miiiichaaaaeeelllll!" Noreen actually lofted through the air toward them.

Allyson managed to duck, but Reuben wasn't so fortunate, and they both went under.

Beyond conscious control, Allyson's body drove for the shore. *Out! Out! Out!* was the only thought in her head.

Except, at the shore, exactly in her way, stood Colonel Michael Gibson with his arms crossed over his chest. He then pointed back into the pool where Noreen and Reuben were sorting themselves out, but neither had their feet under them even though the water wasn't that deep.

In fact, Reuben was drifting toward the outlet stream while he tried to choke out the water he'd swallowed.

Gibson's gesture left no question.

She lunged for Reuben's foot, but the chilled muscles left her attempt well short, and he was gone down the outlet.

Someone grabbed her own foot as she prepared to lunge again.

Noreen.

Allyson kicked hard to shake her off, and was also sucked into the rapids.

She and Reuben were soon rushing downstream.

Just as she caught up to him, a bright yellow bag arced through the air ahead of them. As it flew, it spilled out a line.

She managed to get one arm across Reuben's chest in a swimmer's carry she didn't know she remembered from a summer as lifeguard at the community pool. He continued to choke and spew, but he didn't struggle. With the other, she snagged the rope.

"Roll to get it over your outside shoulder. Left shoulder! Left shoulder!" Someone was shouting at her.

She managed to flip it over her head just as it tightened.

On the bank, she caught a glimpse of one of this morning's horse riders with the rope wrapped around their horse's saddle pommel. With that end anchored, she and Reuben swung like a pendulum from mid-river to hard against the shore. The horse backed up and increased the pressure of the arc until she could barely hold on.

They crawled out of the water, through the half-frozen mud, and flopped onto the brittle grass.

Another line arced out into the river, and seconds later Noreen was lying and spluttering beside them.

The three of them burrowed together for warmth as the shakes set in.

6

"WHO WANTS TO START WITH WHAT YOU COULD HAVE DONE better?" Colonel Gibson now sat across the fire as the three of them huddled as close as they dared.

They were wrapped in somewhat scratchy horse blankets and each had a mug of hot chocolate. Noreen had the added bonus of Xavier wrapping her in his arms from behind.

Reuben was careful not to glance at Allyson. Not that he had any extra warmth to give her, but Noreen and Xavier certainly looked happy together.

"We could have k-k-killed you before you p-pushed us in!" Allyson snapped it out.

Reuben had to laugh.

"Go-od luck with th-th-that," Noreen stuttered out. "He's the f-f-former commander and the most decorated shol—sol-dier in Delta Force history."

Allyson didn't hesitate for a second. Still glaring at the colonel, "They teach you how to be faster than a bullet?"

"No. Smarter than one though."

"Smarter than a lump of lead. Yeah, that's mighty grand."

"That'll do," Gibson's tone changed enough to shut them all up.

Even Allyson, though Reuben was half-tempted to egg her on. She was fun even if she didn't smile much.

"I should have grabbed Reuben and Noreen right away, the moment they entered the water," Allyson grumbled out. "Might have saved us a ride down the river."

"That's one," Gibson nodded.

"You shouldn't have kicked me," Noreen added. "That put two people into the rapids instead of one."

Allyson stuttered out a sigh, drank some chocolate, then nodded.

Gibson held up the lead rope from a stuff bag at his feet. "You handled the rope well. Do you remember what was shouted at you?"

Reuben had been too busy drowning to pay much attention to anything. Allyson and Noreen checked in with each other but neither answered.

"Okay. We'll cover it in the classroom. But for the pendulum to work, the rope is best over the outside shoulder. If the victim has it pinned to their inside shoulder, it will tend to roll them face down into the water. What else worked?"

"Having the ropes there in the first place?" Reuben tried not to make it a question, but Gibson was a seriously daunting dude.

"Exactly. The rope, plus a backup in this case to rescue Noreen. There are techniques to reuse the other end of the same rope if time is tight, which we'll show you."

Allyson dumped the last of her cocoa in the fire and chucked the mug aside. "What you're saying is that I should have had them land the CSAR helicopter in hostile territory. Climbed out into the jungle, and cast a rope to a probably incapacitated soldier in the hopes that he would grab it before he was washed over a waterfall, and fall thirty meters onto a boulder field. Thanks. That's real fucking helpful."

Gibson just waited out her entire tirade.

When she was done, she looked even more drained than she had on the bench this morning. She rested her face on her pulled-up knees.

Reuben rubbed a comforting hand up and down her back. Well, at least her burst of fury had stopped the shivers that still twitched along his own spine.

"No, Sergeant Allyson Hanover. I'm saying that we've just shown you one technique for swiftwater rescue with a rope. We're going to go through every known technique. And then we'll start experimenting with what can be incorporated into CSAR heli-operations. We don't know. None of us has ever tried this before."

Reuben was the only one close enough to hear her curse into her knees.

"What?"

"It means we're going *back into the water.*"

Reuben's shivers, which had faded while he concentrated on the feel of Allyson's back beneath his palm, returned.

7

THE COMBINED CREWS OF THE TWO HELICOPTERS AND ALL THE ranch hands were too numerous for the cozy seating around the kitchen fireplace. So, while the uninvolved ranchers and a fair passel of children stayed there, the rest of them gathered in the ranch's main living room.

The massive fireplace of rounded river rock would have dominated any lesser room. The timber-beam cathedral ceiling was lost in the shadows above. The towering windows glowed with the last of the October sunset.

It was little surprise to her that she and the other two medics ended up sitting on the broad flat-stone shelf close by the fire. After the morning's first plunge, they'd been given fresh clothes and insulated Mustang float suits, the kind that kept Alaskan fisherman alive if they were tossed into the Bering Sea. But at least the fishermen wouldn't be tossed in again. And again. And again.

Despite the neoprene suits, Allyson wondered when she'd ever be truly warm...again.

The fire close by her back was convincing her of "maybe."

Mark and Emily were on one couch with a pair of girls at their feet—one playing dolls, and the other flying in with occasional forays from her air force of tiny diecast aircraft.

Another pair, the dog trainers, were marked for easy reference by a pair big Malinois sleeping across their feet.

The trio of horsewomen were missing. They'd gleefully declared a "Girls night out!" and stayed at the remote fishing cabin.

Then there was Colonel Gibson cradling a sleeping young child as if he hadn't been a brutal hard-ass all day.

Once they'd donned the suits, he had led them through several eddy current rescue scenarios. Then phalanx rescue, where a team formed a triangle and held onto each other for support as they forged into a strong current. Daisy chain crossings, where one person moved into the water, then another came around through the slack water below to be one step farther across the stream, then another joined. This way, the front line could simply brace, and the one person on the move was in calmer water to reach the victim.

Then they'd advanced to "helpless" techniques, where the victim was incapacitated.

A CSAR swimmer cutting far enough across the river to put the line, not the swimmer, in front of the victim. It would snag them, creating a deep-V in the line, and then they could be secured by the swimmer cutting back across the river on the victim's upstream side.

They also learned two-line techniques that auto-formed lassoes around victims, and a dozen more.

"Now," Gibson pulled her back to full awareness just before she fell asleep against the warm hearthstones. "Tell us."

A small burst of panic adrenaline slapped aside her

drowsiness. Telling this tale to the debriefers or Reuben had been one thing. Telling it in front of so many Army officers —even if Beale, Henderson, and Gibson were retired—was something else entirely.

But there was nothing for it, so she leaned into the traces, and told the story again. No one interrupted, except for a brief dive-bomb attack by a toy 747 taking on a bright blue frog. The outcome was inconclusive until a large orange teddy bear put a decisive end to the battle.

"Again," Gibson insisted.

She raised her eyebrows at him. He raised them right back. *Shit!*

This time he interrupted her so often that she had trouble keeping track of the sequence of events.

"Who decided to put the helicopter sideways across the current?"

Allyson tried to remember, but couldn't. "It wasn't me. But it made perfect sense. Captain Berman got our cargo deck almost down to the water. It was an easy reach to grab the swimmer."

Emily groaned as if in pain. Mark looked equally unhappy.

"What?"

Emily took a deep breath. "How high was the cargo deck above the water flow?"

"Inch or two. I didn't exactly have time to get out a ruler and check. But we ended up with occasional flow across the deck."

The two of them glanced at each other, but it was Emily who explained. "The underbelly of a Black Hawk is thin, but not non-existent. If your deck was flush with the water, then the belly was pushed perhaps a foot *into* the water.

That would create an area of accelerated flow rate, an undertow—like an upside-down Venturi flow over a wing. Even with the winch, you might have had trouble pulling him free from the increased water pressure. Rather than helping you haul him up on the edge of the cargo deck, it sucked the soldier out of your grasp and beneath the helo."

Allyson pictured it. "That's what felt wrong. As soon as I leaned out and grabbed him, I could feel the drag pulling at him more than made sense from just the river current. I almost got dragged out, too. Would have been if I hadn't lost my grip."

Reuben touched her arm. "Which secure point did you use for your Monkey Tail line?"

Allyson looked up and tried to remember the configuration of the Black Hawk's cargo deck ceiling rather than that of the vaulted oak beams lost in firelight, and the darkness of night now outside the ranch's big windows.

"Uh, door center. Chief Thompson was latched into the D-ring at the exact center of the deck area."

His hand tightened on her arm.

For a second she wondered why, then she felt a chill as sharp as any she'd felt today, and was thankful for his grounding touch.

"If I'd held my grip—" As a fellow medic, Reuben would understand how hard she'd tried to do that.

"You'd have been towed under the helo as well. Then you'd have been trapped under there by your Monkey Tail just as assuredly as the soldier was by the winch cable."

"Bloody hell," Major Lang whispered softly. "I'd have made that same choice myself, landing across the current."

"Well," Gibson said without any inflection she could detect, "we now know that isn't the correct choice."

"So what is?"

"We'll figure that out tomorrow."

"Great," Reuben's whisper was close enough to her ear to almost tickle. "That means we're *back in the water.*"

It did.

8

"WE'VE ALREADY DROPPED THE YURTS AND SHUT DOWN MOST of the cabins for the season," Mark had announced. "Who's okay in the bunkhouse?"

There were enough cabins still open for all of the couples. Lang, Maloney, and Roberts shared another— already deep in pilot chatter as they headed out the door.

That left two each of both the Chinook and Black Hawk crews, Allyson, and Reuben himself for the bunkhouse.

The two crews peeled off the hallway at the first two rooms.

Reuben was just ahead when he reached the last room and looked in at the bunk beds.

"Um, Allyson. Are you okay with sharing a room? There don't seem to be any others." She looked even more tired than he felt. Actually, it was still three in the afternoon in Japan, but he'd only spent an hour of the last thirty-six in an actual bed. He was either wide awake or ready to start hallucinating.

Suddenly he wondered if he *was* hallucinating.

Allyson hadn't even bothered to answer. She'd simply

dumped her bag on a chair, then stripped down to panties. The Army t-shirt and sports bra came off. He could only stare at the view, from the back, thank Yahweh, before she pulled on a larger t-shirt and crawled into the lower bunk. She faced the wall, and pulled the heavy red-and-black woven blanket most of the way over her head.

"I'll take that for a yes," as soon as he got his breath back and remembered how to move.

He and Allyson had been thrown together any number of times during the day's exercises. Sometimes rescuing each other, sometimes lying on the grass or cold mud, choking out water and gasping for breath.

Through the day he'd admired her steadiness, her resilience, and her indefatigable commitment. After the initial foray, each time Gibson ordered them back into the water, she was always the first in while he was still trying to wrap his mind around the fact that they weren't done yet. And she was always last out. Not until he and Noreen were fished out as well.

Allyson J. Hanover had no speed setting for "just hold on a sec."

But until this moment, despite how often they'd been in each other's arms, she hadn't really registered as a woman. Let alone such an attractive one. Together, they'd been Night Stalker medics pushing through a hard exercise, like a thousand times before.

Now?

Shit, man! Chances of getting sleep in the same room with her? She reminded him of just how long a dry spell Japan had been for him.

He killed the light, and was down to jockeys and t-shirt himself when she spoke.

"Reuben?" barely more than a whisper.

He stopped with one foot on the ladder to the upper bunk. The wood was smooth from decades of ranch hands making the same climb.

"Do you think I killed him?"

"How can you even ask that?" he planted both feet back on the cold floor.

"If only I'd known not to let them turn the helo sideways, he might—"

"No! We don't even know yet what works. *That's why* we're doing this."

She was silent for long enough that he started to climb again. He made it two steps this time.

"Emily knew. The instant I told her what we did, she knew. Her husband, too."

"So they knew. That doesn't mean you should have. They're two of the best helo pilots in Night Stalker history, have at least a decade on us, and they live on a real live working ranch. They have experiences we don't. Just let it go, and get some sleep."

"I can't!" It wasn't some complaint. It was pain ripped from an agony somewhere deep inside the most determined woman he'd ever met.

It was a pain that no medic could turn away from.

He dropped back to the floor, and sat on the edge of her bunk. Just as they'd started at the riverside fire this morning, he ran a soothing hand over her blanket-covered back. Except this time, she wasn't shivering with cold, but rather with pain.

He lay down on the blanket, wrapping his arm around her waist. She clamped a fold of blanket over his arm to keep him in place. He slipped his other arm under the pillow and earned himself a face full of lush hair that smelled vaguely of fire smoke but mostly of fresh river water.

She hung on long enough for him to register that the room wasn't exactly warm. Freeing his arm from her waist for a moment, he managed to snag the blanket from the upper bunk and drape it over both of them.

It was heavy weaving, probably as geometrically ornate as the one he was holding around Allyson.

"I'm sorry," she whispered somewhere in the vicinity of his elbow as he took over a small corner of the pillow, soft with lush hair.

"Are you Jewish?"

"No. I'm not much of anything, I guess. Why?"

"Well, take if from a Jew who knows. If you aren't Jewish, you don't get to feel so guilty about everything you can't control."

"Sorr—"

"Cut it out, Allyson. I'm serious."

She made a couple of false starts.

He took the liberty of pulling them more tightly together, with the first blanket still between them.

Then she was quiet for long enough that he wondered if she'd gone to sleep.

Until he was drifting off himself from pure and simple exhaustion.

"There's something very wrong with you, Reuben."

It took him a while to wake up enough to speak. "Uh-huh." And a while more before he managed to find his brain sufficiently to mumble, "What?"

Through the blanket, she patted his hand where it was still hooked around her waist. "Never mind. Go to sleep."

It was the last thing he remembered.

9

"So, what's wrong with me?"

"Huh?" Allyson wasn't sure what anything had to do with anything. For one, she woke up in a man's arms. But not. There was still a blanket between them.

Then she remembered how she got into this position and buried her face under the covers to hide the blush that was searing her cheeks. She'd gotten here by being a complete trainwreck.

"Last night, as we were falling asleep, you said there was something wrong with me."

"No, I said *very* wrong."

"Why?"

"When was the last time you slept with a woman without even going for a good grope?" And she buried her face further out of sight. She *hadn't* just said that.

"Hmm. Good question. Let's see. Not since...last night."

"Ha. Ha. Ha."

She could feel his shrug through the blanket. "Didn't seem like what you needed."

Which he'd absolutely gotten right. Allyson had never

been one for mind-numbing sex. She'd been in no shape to sleep—pass out from exhaustion maybe—but not just sleep. Yet in his arms she'd had one of her best nights since Colombia.

"I'd offer to give you a good grope right now if you'd like, but the mice are stirring."

"Mice?" she peeked out from under the covers in time to see Reuben nodding toward the wall.

Then she heard the rest of the crew getting in motion down the hall.

Reuben rolled away from her, and was half dressed by the time she thought to look. He looked very soldier fit.

He finished while she watched, then he leaned back against the door and crossed his arms.

"What?"

"You watched to make sure I got dressed properly, I'm just returning the favor." His smile was as innocent as a puppy's, but she'd believe that for not even a tenth of a second.

Fine! She threw back the two blankets. "Hey, these are beautiful." They weren't blankets, they were works of art that happened to be used on beds. The geometric pattern in red, black, and buff was simple, yet also mesmerizing.

"Mark's...Major Henderson's mom is a weaver. I asked about some of the throws on the couches." He showed no signs of going away so that she could change.

"What are you really doing?"

"Really?" Reuben managed to keep the innocent look. "I'm trying to see if you're as incredibly beautiful as you were when you undressed right in front of me last night."

"I didn't!" Yet there on the chair were her bra and yesterday's shirt. "I did."

"Back only, but it's a nice physique you have there, Sergeant Allyson Hanover."

"Likewise, Sergeant Reuben Fehlman." Appreciating the tip, she kept her back to him again as she changed. "Well?" she asked when she turned to him.

He slipped fingers up against his own neck, "Pulse rate up over thirty points. Respiration at least plus ten over norm. I don't have a blood pressure cuff handy, but, yeah, that worked for me. You?" And he slipped his fingers against *her* neck to rest under her chin just behind her windpipe. "What's your normal?"

"Sixty," she lied by ten.

"You're up at least fifteen."

No way was her pulse rate running at seventy-five instead of her normal fifty, over having Reuben just touch her. She took a slow calming breath, driving it downward.

"Sixty-five. Which tells me your resting is lower still. Liar! Liar! Pants on fire!" Then he looked down at her sharply.

"What? My pants are *not* on fire."

"I was just making sure. I don't know my own power sometimes. I mean I did just get you mostly naked right here in front of me. And Moses, Abraham, and Isaiah it was amazing. You have exceptional dorsal muscle definition, Sergeant Hanover."

And before she could think of how to answer that, he was out the door and greeting the others in the hall.

She tossed his blanket back onto the upper bunk, then snapped her own into shape before following him.

Her pulse rate was *not* going to escalate over some handsome guy just because he was being nice.

That was totally wack.

10

"How's the old pulse rate now?" He reached out and checked Allyson's pulse.

"Dead man." She lay splatted out on the muddy bank beside him like a beached perch—one pretty well done with flopping.

"While that's a fairly accurate assessment of my condition. Yours is still good. And the wet look definitely works on you."

"I don't have follicles anymore, I have icicles."

They still had on their float suits, but they only wore bicycle-style safety helmets for these exercises. The electronics of flight helmets weren't designed for swimming.

"Will you two just get a hotel room already?" Noreen mumbled somewhere nearby.

"I tried," Allyson heaved out a long-suffering sigh. "Not even a decent grope. Not even a little one."

Noreen smacked the back of his head, almost hard enough to drive Reuben's face into the mud as well.

"I was being a gentleman."

"There's gentleman then there's just plain thickheaded."

Allyson offered him a seraphic smile at Noreen's answer.

"What are we missing?" Reuben pushed up to a sitting position and went for a subject change because one Jewish medic against the force of two Night Stalker women was not a scenario he'd be winning any time soon.

"A hot shower with a man willing to offer at least a good grope," Allyson muttered. But she too sat up, and glared at the landing helicopters.

All morning they'd been the test subjects for how water moved around a hovering helicopter. They'd tried floating buoys down the river but they'd been too light, too susceptible to the massive downblast of wind from the rotors. No, they'd needed to send people. Them.

And what they'd learned was that most of the profiles were terrible.

Head-on into the current, a Black Hawk pushed the water to either side rather than just downward. But, after passing the narrowed nose, the water pressure swept the victim wide, out of reach from the cargo bay doors.

Also, while the rear rotor didn't get too close to the water for flight safety, it was terrifying to be swept past instant death spinning mere feet above the water.

The Chinook, with both of its rotors mounted on top, had seemed like an obvious solution. As a bonus, it was able to turn tail and lower its rear cargo ramp into the water while hovering. SEALs raced loaded Zodiac boats aboard partially submerged Chinooks in a maneuver called Delta Queen.

It did work well enough with floating victims, in the slower parts of the stream. But as soon as they escalated to faster swiftwater, they were swept away to either side except with the most carefully controlled approach.

They hadn't come up with any innovative ideas by the time they were called to lunch.

Chelsea, Julie, and Lauren were the three horsewomen who had ridden out the morning before and had helped with the ropes. Today, other than tossing the recovery line for each failed experiment, they'd had little to do with the test.

Instead, they'd spread a feast around the campfire. BBQ chicken, potato salad, and bear-meat hot dogs abounded.

"Bear meat?" Reuben hadn't thought about bears. "Very few of those in Brooklyn. Or southern Japan for that matter."

"We don't hunt them," Julie the blonde patted the rifle holstered in the saddle she was using as a backrest. "But sometimes they hunt us and won't take no for an easy answer. Especially not now. This far into the fall, they're fattening themselves up for the winter. Mostly trout, late berries, and nuts. But really? Anything they can find. Small animals, carrion, the occasional backpacker." Her grimace said that really happened sometimes.

"I dunno," Lauren the brunette took another chicken wing and dunked it in the sauce that Reuben had discovered was three-alarm-fire hot, and had been avoiding ever since. "Tourist meat for the bears. I think we're missing a real market."

"No!" Chelsea the redhead squealed as if disgusted. "Tourists are all gristly this late in the season. You need to get them in the spring when they still have their winter meat on them. Besides, that's when the grizzlies come out of hibernation all hungry and need the extra calories. Poor little things." Okay, not disgusted, but disgust*ing* perhaps.

The three women started to riff on the best tourists to turn into meat for bears by home country and season.

"No! No! Bear meat tastes of whatever they've eaten. Feed them salmon, they taste all fishy. Living on berries? They're sweet. So, if you feed them a Russian, they're going to taste like vodka. Too strong for me." Chelsea shook her head. "I wonder if Nepalese would taste like Assam tea. I certainly drank a lot of tea the year I spent hiking there."

Reuben looked at the all-American redhead, complete with freckles. A year hiking in Nepal? It was clear you could never judge someone by their cover.

His bear dog was a little gamey, but it had been expertly spiced. The fresh-baked crusty sourdough roll with stone ground mustard was great.

"So what don't I know about you?" He turned to Allyson.

She eyed him over the chicken breast she'd been devouring at a rate only someone who'd spent the whole morning plunging into a glacial river could.

"I actually know very little about you—beyond you like having a good grope in the mornings."

"You missed your evening opportunity as well."

"Damn! I guess I did. Okay, I'll trade you one for one. I come from a Jewish family that wanted a doctor, lawyer, or banker. They got all three: my three older sisters. Which let me be a total failure by becoming an Army medic. I'm happy, but they barely let me slip in the door for Passover along with the spirit of Elijah."

"Elijah?"

"Fancy prophet. Likes a glass of wine once a year. Insists on having his own special glass though. That's two you owe me."

She watched him long enough to consume another big bite of the chicken breast. "My family has a legacy of working in steel mills. Except the mills closed forty years ago. They're still on the couch waiting in their trailers for them to come back."

No hint of a smile to tell him it was a joke.

"Okay, part two, why isn't that you?"

Allyson glanced around as if searching for an answer. Apparently not finding one, she shrugged before answering.

"I'm guess I'm not very patient."

She went back to eating her chicken.

11

JODI AND STAN'S DOGS OFFERED A WELCOME BREAK.

The two humans were juggernaut types—*I'm going this way and nothing is going to stop me*—and Stan was big and broad-shouldered enough to actually be one. Jodi just had the can-do attitude of one.

Allyson decided that she wouldn't mind being just like them.

Their dogs had an absolute willingness to dive out of helicopters into any type of water. They thought swimming in rushing, sub-Arctic waters was a complete lark.

If the victim was capable of grabbing onto the dogs' harnesses, then they were quickly dragged to safety. The dogs were equally willing to take directions from a heli-bound handler or a victim; they were a wonder to work with.

But if the victim was incapacitated, then it started to break down.

The dogs had been trained to bite onto the shoulder of a vest.

However, unlike dragging a heavy person over the

ground while going backwards, dogs only swam forward. They could latch onto the victim or they could swim—they couldn't do both.

By the time they gave up, both dogs were bedraggled and very frustrated.

To make them feel better, Allyson jumped in a few times and let them come rescue her—dragging her along as she held onto their harnesses.

Reuben did a neat backflip off the rear ramp of the Chinook, which also delighted the dogs who dove in after him, and raced downstream to catch up.

"School dive team," he told her.

"Volleyball team." He'd looked at her five-eight askance. "I never said I was good."

"Oh, like I believe that." It had earned her one of his good laughs. She was getting to enjoy how easily he did that. She wished it was contagious, but laughing had never been one of her things.

"Okay, caught me. I was a wicked setter, but the rest of the team pretty much sucked—we were more of a softball and soccer school for the girls—so we didn't win much anyway."

Again the laugh, that made her feel included rather than sidelined.

With both the floating to the helo and the dog tests being mostly failures, they called it a day.

Back at the ranch, Allyson just let herself deep soak under the hot shower.

Nothing had yet worked. She still felt that soldier slipping out of her fingers like a bar of wet soap every time she closed her hands. She couldn't depend on the near-perfect timing Crew Chief Thompson had shown the moment before he died. A half second slower or an inch off, and the soldier would have been gone completely rather than caught on the winch cable.

She supposed that was the one solace in the whole situation. If they hadn't managed to get the winch cable attached, the wounded (or perhaps dead) soldier would have been swept past, over the waterfall, and would surely have died on the rocks below. It also would have meant a closed-coffin funeral.

"You in here?" Reuben called into the bunkhouse bathroom.

"No!"

"I'll take that as a yes." She could hear the good cheer in Reuben's tone.

"You just want another excuse to see me naked," she called out as she finished her last rinse.

This time she heard the laugh. "Well, I sure wouldn't mind. But I was actually going to ask if you minded having a naked man in the next shower stall over."

"I've been in the Army for over eight years. Trust me, I'm used to it."

"Okay."

And she didn't hear anything else until the shower next to hers turned on. They were separated by one of those steel panels, just like bathroom stalls, and all she could see of him were his bare feet below the bottom edge.

He started singing, in a decent baritone, that echoed off the bathroom walls. "*Splish Splash, I was takin' a shower. Long about*—what is this? Tuesday?—*Tuesday night. A rub dub, I was looking for a rhyme to dub, thinkin' everything was alright.*"

He made sputtering sounds as he kept singing, and she saw soap rinsing down his feet and across the tile floor toward their shared drain.

She reached her hand over the barrier, and squirted a

stream of shampoo at him. Apparently it found its target as he began sputtering and cursing instead of sputtering and singing.

Allyson shut off her own shower, dried, dressed, and got out of there before he was done.

She might not be laughing, but she was definitely smiling.

12

Reuben stood at the bunkhouse room door, and considered his next action.

He'd gotten to talking with Stan the dog guy about his artificial arm. He'd never seen anything like it.

"Newest tech out of Stonybrook. Got a professor there who thinks I'm the perfect guinea pig." He grunted thoughtfully. "Guess I am." He then demonstrated how accurately he could control the arm. "Fully tapped into the old nerves up in my biceps. Pressure and heat. Your hand is warm when I shake it, and I can feel that I'm not crushing down on you."

Then he'd stroked his fingertips over his wife's cheek. "Or how lightly I'm touching you." Despite the brutal scars on the side of his face, his expression softened so much that Reuben had felt embarrassed for intruding.

That's when he'd missed Allyson.

He did a quick fade but didn't find her anywhere in the ranch house. Following a guess, he'd traced her back to their room. Once again curled up facing the wall on the lower bunk, asleep to all appearances.

That's when he noticed two very key facts.

First, not only were her bra and Army t-shirt folded neatly on the chair by the foot of the bed, so was the shirt she'd slept in last night.

Second, even though the room wasn't particularly cold, both blankets were spread over the lower bunk.

Not being a fool, well, not always, he stripped down and slipped in beside her.

This time, when he put his arm around her bare waist, the shiver he felt had nothing to do with the cold. She felt so warm and alive it was hard to credit.

Allyson Hanover was all about the business of rescue in the field.

But watching her play with the dogs in the river had practically been a revelation. The serious medic had cavorted with them until even the dogs were tired. For the final rescue, he'd thrown her in, then dived after her. They'd clasped hands and let the two dogs come and rescue them together. She'd still been holding his hand when they collapsed exhausted on the riverbank and just lay there watching a hawk wheeling across the impossibly blue sky.

At least until one of the dogs had licked him in the face.

Also, the playful shampoo attack in the shower. She'd totally missed. But in his surprise that Allyson *had* unwound enough to do such a thing, he'd inhaled a mouthful of dribbling water. She'd been gone by the time he'd finished choking it out of his lungs.

The same Allyson, who had joked about him *not* groping her.

Well, he wasn't going to set himself up for the complaint again.

He slid up a hand to cradle one of her breasts—a perfect handful. She sighed happily, and pushed back against him.

The rest of their first time together passed just that way: slow, silent, and glorious.

13

"How about this?" Julie, the blonde horsewoman, spun a lasso over her head. With a perfect cast, it flew out into the water, landed neatly over Noreen's raised arm, and slid tight.

"Wow!" Allyson couldn't believe how perfect it looked; it was a move right out of those longhorn cattle movies. "How long did it take you to learn that?"

The redheaded Chelsea offered Julie a hip check that almost tumbled her into the stream. "She won the Calgary Stampede last year. Top barrel racer in the world."

"Well, in Calgary anyway." Julie gathered her wet line, then answered Allyson's question. "It takes a while, but it's not impossible like being a medic or something."

"Don't believe her. In rodeo, Calgary *is* the *entire* world. Can't swing that rope in a helicopter though." Chelsea frowned, an unusual expression for her. "Is there some kind of a lasso gun?"

No one had heard of one...except Colonel Gibson.

"There is one. It fires out a Kevlar string and wraps around the victim like a bola throwing weapon. It will pin the arms or legs, but it wouldn't work if it hit water. This is about swiftwater rescue, not non-lethal restraint."

But the idea did start her on a series of experiments.

The heaved rope bag from their first rescue was defeated by the downblast of wind from the rotors. It proved almost impossible to get any distance on a sideways throw. There was also the question of a bad throw possibly getting caught up in the rotor blades. That would be unbelievably bad news.

However, a dragged line proved promising.

Using a rope bag as a sort of sea anchor, she dropped one end of the line in the slow-moving water along the bank. Ordering the helo sideways across the river, she was able to spool out line in front of the victim as if the helo itself was the thrown rope bag.

Within the hour, she was able to make the calls to the pilots Maloney and Major Lang to complete and precise line-setting.

Soon she was consistently capturing Reuben and Noreen as they floated down the river.

Rougher water decreased the effectiveness, but it was still high. Everyone in the group started cheering and offering up suggestions.

They even brought the dogs back out, testing them diving in and swimming around a non-responsive victim to get them snagged in a loop. That ultimately failed because as soon as the rope tightened, the dog was dragged inexorably into the victim. If they were in panic, they could easily drown the dog without realizing what they were doing.

It was Major Lang who solved how to lay the line to encircle an incapacitated victim.

"It's a strange maneuver from the cockpit. We're flying

most of it blind, where we can't see the victim. But once you have the feel for it..." her shrug looked pleased.

She had Allyson attach the anchoring bag in the middle of the line and drop it. Then, as before, they crossed the river downstream from the victim. The moment before the victim hit the lines, Allyson would call "Circle Line."

Major Lang didn't *steer* the helicopter in a circle. Instead, she used the rudders to spin the helo on its axis, spinning the tail to swing away from the bag. The main rotor was above the front of the wide cargo door. So, if Allyson trailed one line out the leading edge of the door, it essentially stayed in place as the helicopter twisted on its axis.

But the line she trailed out the back of the door would loop neatly around behind the victim. Then, with a slip knot already tied around the primary line, she'd let go of the aft one.

It snaked down and made a perfect lasso around the victim.

By mid-afternoon they could do it every time from the Black Hawk and over half the time from the big Chinook.

Lunch was a complete celebration.

Allyson wondered if she looked as goofy as Reuben and Noreen—neither of them could stop smiling. She supposed so, her cheek muscles ached when she pressed fingers to them.

"Damn but that was amazing, Medic Hanover." Reuben kissed her right in front of everybody.

The only comment she heard over the buzzing in her ears was Noreen's, "About damn time!" and Xavier's, "Hush, woman."

The mood continued until the end of the meal when Gibson called them to order.

"Okay, now for a real test."

14

ALLYSON HAD OFFERED TO BE THE VICTIM, BUT REUBEN refused. He'd tried the rope trick enough to have the technique, but it would be a lot more practice before he'd be as good as Allyson.

As good as Allyson.

There was a laugh. He'd been a medic for the same eight years Allyson had, but when she and Noreen started talking advanced techniques, he could barely follow. In fact, there were times that Noreen looked flummoxed trying to keep up.

Allyson didn't just know how to patch people up; she knew the human body at a level he doubted his sister the general practitioner understood.

As a Night Stalker, she was a shining example of what "giving it your all" meant.

And in bed? Holy Moses she was more than he'd ever dreamed of.

She needed a victim? Definitely let it be him.

Which it turned out she did.

In the Chinook, Gibson flew him up into the mountains

of the Flathead Wilderness that their river had descended from. Noreen rode with them; Allyson was in the Black Hawk trailing far behind just like a real mission.

They passed over a tall cascading waterfall, past a broad lake with a trio of moose wading in the water, and out into the fir trees taller than Brooklyn high rises. Twenty stories tall, clustered so thickly that the river often disappeared from view.

"You ready?" It was so uncharacteristic of Colonel Gibson to ask before shoving him into the water, that he wasn't sure how to respond.

Reuben double-checked that all of the closures on his neoprene float suit were secure, and that his helmet was well seated.

"Ready as I'll ever be." Reuben swung his legs off the back edge of the lowered rear cargo ramp, ready to drop into the river ten feet below. The heavy beating of the rotor close overhead meant they had to shout to be overheard. The downdraft was flattening the tops of the rapids below, but Reuben could see it would be a fast-and-wild ride.

Gibson, rather than slapping him on the back as good to go, kept a hand solidly on his shoulder.

Reuben looked at him. Gibson was watching him closely.

"Ready as you'll ever be..." He didn't seem to like the words as he repeated them.

"Yeah."

"That," Gibson looked as if he'd bitten down on something sour, "is *not* how you win the love of a Night Stalker."

For half a second, he thought Gibson was speaking a little metaphorically about himself. Then realized that he was speaking very literally about Allyson.

Love?

In love with Allyson?

Maybe not today, but... He'd sure as hell never met anyone like her. Sure he never would.

But maybe someday? Yeah, definitely. Which almost made him in love with her already by definition? But that meant—

"So how *do* you win the love of a Night Stalker?" He'd seen the Delta Force colonel with his Night Stalker wife and their kid. He was a man who knew.

"Night Stalkers Don't Quit. It's your motto. Night Stalkers don't know how to. You've got to be at that level. Not just in the field, but with the woman. You commit, and you don't quit."

Then he shoved Reuben hard between the shoulder blades, and he was falling into frigid waters.

15

"Victim in the water! I repeat: Victim in the water!"

Allyson felt the cold sweat in her palms as the call came over the radio. It was the first call she'd gotten in the month since Colombia, and it brought back a flood of memories. Bad ones.

This might be only an exercise, but could she be good enough?

Last night she almost hadn't left the invitation for Reuben. He was a little...too...normal? Too nice for a screwed up mess like her?

Yet no matter how exhausted they were, he'd kept his humor. And he'd kept pushing like a hardened soldier.

Each time she'd been ready to descend into doubt, he'd been there to stop that, too.

That first night, without calling her childish or naive, he'd quashed her guilt trip by just asking, *How can you even think that?* And then he'd held her like she was stronger and smarter than she knew she was. Since then, she'd been too embarrassed to admit such foolish fears to a man so...steady.

And last night. He'd made love to her as if *she* was the important one.

Nobody had ever made her feel that way.

And now some totally irrational part of her brain connected: *Victim in the water,* Reuben, and the dead soldier dangling from the end of a winch cable.

Telling herself it was just an exercise, and that Reuben was *not* the dead soldier, didn't help as much as it should.

As the Black Hawk raced up into the Montana wilderness to locate him, Allyson went through the rote steps.

Her med kits hung on the rear cargo net, though she hadn't zippered them open, because this was just an exercise.

Dammit!

She doubled back and did. If it was a combat exercise, she was going to treat it like one. A glance showed that all of her med gear was in place.

It took a moment's debate between snapping the Monkey Tail at the cabin's center or out over the door edge. She finally went for the extra reach of being snapped into the door edge. After all, they weren't doing dunk-the-rescue-helo techniques anymore.

This time, she had a single-rope and a double-rope bag set close to hand. Next time she'd add a bungy cord to hold them in place against the hard turns the helo was carving along the river.

She and Crew Chief Xavier Jones checked each other's lines, then she slid open the cargo bay door, and made sure that it latched. Again.

Together, they leaned out to study the river below.

The situation was both like and unlike Colombia.

The towering trees were dark conifer green beneath a

sparkling sun, rather than tangled and towering jungle painted in muted apple-green tones by night vision. The temperature was far from tropical, but after so many immersions in the icy river, she didn't notice it much.

Like the jungle, the fir trees often hid stretches of the rushing river. It was only at occasional pools that it slowed and widened enough for a helicopter to safely descend to the water. And even then, they were still moving rapidly.

"Victim in sight," she and Major Lang made the call simultaneously.

The bright orange float suit was racing down through the narrow passage of rapids. Reuben was in the "defensive float" posture—on his back, and feet first—that offered both best vision ahead and the ability to push off a rock before hitting it with your head.

"Pool fifty meters east."

"Too soon," Lang reported back. "He'll be through before we can get there."

Allyson leaned out enough to scan along the river. "Another a hundred more meters."

"Roger." And with the same gut-wrenching twist that Captain Berman had used, the pilots dove the Black Hawk down toward the second pool, even as Reuben flowed through the first pool.

He looked up and waved.

She tried to wave back, but the trees blocked her view.

16

REUBEN HAD NEVER BEEN WHITEWATER RAFTING BEFORE, BUT he definitely had to try it. Or maybe create a new sport of float-jacketing down major rapids. This stretch was much rougher and faster than any of their practice water. The ride was wild, and seriously adrenaline pumping.

As he'd learned over the last several days, he steered clear of obstacles by using a dragged hand when he could. When it wasn't enough, he did a simple, sideways barrel roll. That placed him out of harm's way any number of times.

This week had been an amazing education.

The victim's-eye view was something he'd never practiced, except when replacing a rescue dummy in some "wounded warrior" exercise. But Gibson had been right to send them into the water. Having a victim's view had drastically modified their tactics for the better. It was also now ingrained into his instincts that you couldn't trust that the victim was able to help themselves.

If Colonel Gibson was right about that, was he also right about winning a Night Stalkers' heart?

He glanced aloft, catching glimpses of the Black Hawk racing above the trees. Allyson was—

Reuben slammed into a "pillow." The swift current, pushing hard against the face of a boulder, drove a narrow envelope upstream and to the sides. It acted as a cushion around the upstream side of the rock and it was all that saved him from a hard battering.

Slipping around the rock, he tumbled into the steep-edged eddy current behind the boulder, and came to an abrupt stop. At least a stop as far as flowing downstream was concerned.

He was in the "hole"—that gap between the rock and the high boil where the downstream flow around either side of the rock collided.

Trapped in the vortex.

The upstream side of the boil current sucked him down into the hole, dragged him downstream, then drove him back to the surface of the boil—only to slide back into the hole again. Without the float suit, he'd be in real trouble.

Pushing off the rock didn't get him free, and the bottom had been scooped out too deeply for him to get any footing.

Shit! Shit! Shit!

He tried to swim up the eddy wall to get back into the main current, but it was too high, driving him back into the hole.

The next time he was driven down, he tried swimming out underneath the boil, but the float suit fought against him, forcing him back to the boil's surface.

This was getting really bad.

A section of a split tree trunk shot into the hole and slammed him in the ribs. It was pure chance that in clutching his side, he also managed to grab the three-foot curved chunk of tree.

Ignoring the pain in his ribs, he tried maneuvering it like a paddle.

Too awkward.

Then he stuck it into the eddy wall and it was almost ripped downstream out of his hands.

Good sign.

The next time he surfaced, he stabbed it high into the wall of the eddy and held on tight. He teetered on the balance, but managed to keep his grip. Between one instant and the next, he was flung out of the hole and back into the main current.

Now, if he was careful, his troubles were over.

17

"He's late. He should be through by now."

No one argued with Allyson's assessment. *Dammit!*

She tried to see upriver, but the trees met over where the rushing river's outlet made a short waterfall. The shadows were too dark compared to the sun shining off the water.

Her hand hovered over the two throwing bags, but she didn't know which would be better until she saw if Reuben was playing incapacitated victim or not.

The main current focused directly beneath them, but so did the sun's reflection. If they... "Ten meters due south if you have the room."

As the helo moved, the angle of the sun shifted.

More and more she could see up into the shadowed tunnel of trees over the river, not that it would let her see someone in the water more than one second sooner. And Reuben was far later than that.

"There!" A bright orange float suit raced toward the outlet.

"I confirm sighting," Xavier reported from close beside her.

Then she saw what was standing at the head of the waterfall—and screamed.

18
———

Nothing!

Nothing could be that big!

Reuben swam desperately for the shore, but the current was too strong.

He couldn't even steer for the riverbank as there was no bank. The water raced through a cut of smooth stone walls.

The float jacket made it impossible to submerge.

As he reached the upper crest of the waterfall, the massive brown grizzly bear raised a paw bigger than his head—and swung.

19

ALLYSON SAW THE BLOW.

Saw Reuben tumble over the waterfall like a lifeless rag doll.

"Back ten," Xavier called from some distant place a lifetime ago.

Reuben was face-up, but floating headfirst through the pool of water.

Making no effort to spin himself around.

Maybe he couldn't.

Then there was a huge splash behind him.

The bear surfaced and began swimming fast toward him as if the helo wasn't even there.

Allyson slapped for her sidearm, but she hadn't put it on for the exercises. Besides, Chelsea told her that a 9mm round would only irritate a bear.

The Black Hawk's Miniguns also weren't loaded. She could see the second crew chief frantically trying to do so.

No time for rope tricks.

"North and down! North and down!" She shouted over the intercom.

Major Lang didn't even hesitate, sliding them sideways towards Reuben.

"All the way down! Into the water!"

"Are you—"

"Down! Now!" Allyson shouted over the intercom. She yanked on the Monkey Tail one last time to make sure it was secure.

Then, with Reuben rushing toward them, and the bear gaining fast—she jumped.

20

REUBEN COULDN'T LOOK AWAY FROM THE BEAR.

Before it had looked the size of a Chinook.

Now it was more like the size of a B-52 come to bomb him out of existence.

Its paw had smashed into the wooden pole Reuben had used to get out of the eddy-current hole, and shattered it against his side. His ribs had exploded with pain. He couldn't seem to breathe.

And now?

Now it was going to—

Something fell on him and drove him underwater.

The bear's paw somehow crashing from above?

Whatever hit him, wrapped around him like legs and arms in a mighty embrace. He prepared for the final crushing blow.

The float suit buoyed him back to the surface one last time.

Someone was shouting in his ears, "Climb! Climb! Climb!"

He floated, dangling in the unlikely embrace.

As the deafening roar of an M134 Minigun unleashed just above his head, the world went black.

21

"NO," REUBEN GROANED. "NO, I *DON'T* WANT TO EAT THE BEAR that almost got me."

"You sure?" Chelsea didn't give up easily. "I mean it seems only fair. He almost had you for lunch. How about a bearskin rug?"

"Respectfully...no!"

"Pity. Anyway, lucky for you Allyson did her flying squirrel trick."

Allyson the flying squirrel?

Reuben started to laugh, then groaned. "Agh! No! No! Do *not* make me laugh." He clutched his side.

The docs at Malmstrom Air Force Base had assured him that while he had plenty of fractured ribs, none of them were actually broken.

They were more worried about the broken tibia and the five long, deep cuts where the bear's talons had actually caught his calf as Allyson had lifted him to safety. But they'd finally declared Allyson's treatment—she'd stitched muscle and skin during the racing flight to the hospital—as being as good as any of them could have done, even if she was in the Army rather than the Air Force.

He'd heard one of the docs asking why she hadn't done med school. If he remembered correctly through the drugs, the question had stumped her, as if she didn't know how to answer. Maybe she hadn't ever thought to look that high. Maybe he should egg her on.

The Chinook had delivered the dead bear back to the ranch before returning to JBLM. The Black Hawk had waited at the hospital, then flown him the thirty minutes back to the ranch where nothing was too good for him.

He now lay comfortably sprawled on a couch close by the big fire with the Black Hawk's other crew and the ranchers gathered around. The only thing he really cared about was that his head was resting in Allyson's lap, and her hand was holding his.

"Stop looking so spooked, Medic Hanover. You saved my life. Twice," he lifted his leg cast. Then wished he hadn't because of the pull on his ribs punched at least part way through the painkillers.

"That was seriously out there," Noreen said.

"It was only because—" Allyson was looking down at him and Reuben's breath caught. The idea that she might have risked her life specifically for him was huge.

"Gonna call bullshit on you, girl. I bet you'd have done the same if it was *my* sorry ass the bear was after." Noreen's laugh was really hard not to join in.

Allyson's shrug, he was learning to read those, said "Maybe." As in "Definitely."

"I thought I was the most 'out there' medic in the Night Stalkers, but I'm absolutely passing the title to you. Jumping in between your victim and a grizzly bear so that you could act like a human lifting harness. Seriously extreme."

"That was Khyber Pass-level brave," Major Lang said softly.

Allyson looked up at the major long enough for her to look uncomfortable.

"She, too, made a choice." Noreen pointed a beer bottle at Major Lang from where she slouched in her chair.

"Noreen," Lang groaned and settled into a chair.

"Hell no, you don't get out of this one, Lois. You forget, I was medic on that bird. So, you gonna tell this or am I?"

"I'd never forget that. You're the one who saved my life."

"Guilty," Noreen's smile was easy but the two women shared a look that spoke of a massive bond of respect.

Reuben looked up at Allyson and figured that the same expression was probably on his own face at the moment.

Major Lang continued, "Since you'll embellish it ridiculously, I'll do it."

Noreen's smile shifted and said she'd do exactly that.

Lang turned to face them, then she raised her mechanical foot and plinked it with her finger.

"Sergeant Hanover... Allyson. Like you, I made a choice. No warning. No time for thought. But, as you now understand, it wasn't a choice. I could turn one way, and I'd have walked away from a crash with probably no more than a scrape. Or I could turn the other, which I'm surprised only cost my foot."

"Choose Door Number One!" Reuben winced. "Dumb thing to say. Sorry, ma'am. Drugs speaking."

"No, it isn't. Many pilots make the first choice. Those pilots do not fly CSAR for the 5th Battalion Night Stalkers. There was a cost with the first choice—but there was no time to think about it."

"See?" Noreen called out. "She'd already saved my life,

so I figured I had to save hers, just to keep things even, you know. And this was in a hella-ugly gun battle that—"

Allyson's whisper was soft, but it silenced the room. "The price of your survival was the lives of your crew?"

Major Lang nodded.

Everyone ignored her.

"But it was never a question." Allyson's voice became more certain.

"No more than the moment you leapt out of the helicopter to the end of your safety line to save your victim from that bear."

"NSDQ," Allyson said it softly.

"NSDQ," the major repeated. Noreen, then others around the room echoed the saying in soft whispers.

Talk quieted through the evening as Reuben blurred in and out. The drugs softened the edges of everything. After a brief doze, he came awake to a much smaller fire, and a mostly empty living room.

Only Major Lang remained, talking quietly with Allyson.

"You'll be getting a Soldier's Medal for that particular act of heroism, by the way."

Allyson simply shook her head.

"Hey, Ms. Medic Hanover," Reuben reached up to play with the ends of her hair gone golden in the firelight. "That's huge. Medals don't get any better than a Soldier's outside a combat zone."

When she shook her head again, her face mostly disappeared behind that shower of dark gold.

"She understands," Major Lang's look said that he'd better understand too if he wanted to stay in her outfit.

That was becoming a major priority. He had to find a way to stay in the 5th, just to be near Allyson.

Lang continued, "Neither the Purple Heart nor the Silver Star have anything to do with how I feel about losing my foot. Instead, it's the foot that reminds me of what's important."

He nodded that he finally understood, but everything had suddenly gotten so serious. If Allyson looked any more miserable, he'd be the one to start crying.

"What about me? Huh?" He tugged lightly on Allyson's hair to make sure she was listening. "I'm the one who got mauled by the bear. I could have died. I should get something."

"I think you already got your reward," Major Lang patted his hand, and left them alone by the fire.

"What's she talking about?"

Allyson just shook her head, but she brushed her fingertips along his forehead and down his cheek.

He thought about it, but not awfully hard. The stupid drugs made him...stupid.

So, instead, he looked up into Allyson's face. Her cheeks were glowing more than firelight seemed to account for.

"What reward? I didn't get bear meat."

"You didn't want any."

"I don't get a bearskin rug. Isn't that supposed to be a thing? Naked woman on a bearskin rug?"

She just shook her head again, but he'd teased out her smile.

"I'll bet you'd look exceptional, all naked on a bearskin rug. Is that my reward?"

The smile grew, but again the headshake.

"I don't get it." He didn't mind that the joke was on him, he just hated not knowing the joke in the first place.

Allyson's smile just grew until the strangest thing happened.

She started to laugh.

He smiled in return, but it kept building until it danced along the edge of hysterical.

"What?" No question she was laughing *at* him, not with him.

"You've helped develop a new heli-rescue technique that's going to save lives. You floated down a wild river, were mauled by a bear, and now you're pouting about a reward like a twelve-year-old? It's just a little much."

He stuck out his lower lip and went for his pouty-face.

It earned him another sparkle of laughter.

"I still want my reward," he went for *extreme* pouty-face.

Allyson abruptly sobered and he wondered where he'd gone wrong. What trigger had he hit this time, like that very first conversation up on the knoll-top bench?

She lifted her hand from his cheek and rested it on his chest. On his bandages.

No.

Over his heart.

He looked up at her.

Oh! *That* was his reward. And the major was right, it was far beyond any mere medal.

Then he rested his hand over hers.

She'd rescued him... No, while fighting the swiftwater, they'd rescued each other in more ways than he could count.

Night Stalkers didn't know how to quit.

That meant that this rescue had the *best* kind of reward, a lifelong one.

TARGET OF THE HEART
(EXCERPT)

IF YOU ENJOYED THAT, BE SURE YOU
DON'T MISS THE 5E SERIES!

TARGET OF THE HEART (EXCERPT)

PETE'S CHINOOK AND HIS TWO ESCORT BLACK HAWKS crossed into the mountainous province of Sikkim, India ten feet over the glaciers and still moving fast. It was an hour before dawn, they'd made it out of China while it was still dark.

"Thirty minutes of fuel remaining," Nicolai said it like a personal challenge when they hit the border.

"Thanks, I never would have noticed."

It had been a nail-biting tradeoff: the more fuel he burned, the more easily he climbed due to the lighter load. The more he climbed, the faster he burned what little fuel remained.

Safe in Indian airspace he climbed hard as Nicolai counted down the minutes remaining, burning fuel even faster than he had been while crossing the mountains of southern Tibet. They caught up with the U.S. Air Force HC-130P Combat King refueling tanker with only ten minutes of fuel left.

"Ram that bitch," Nicolai called out.

Pete extended the refueling probe which reached only a

few feet beyond the forward edge of the rotor blade and drove at the basket trailing behind the tanker on its long hose.

He nailed it on the first try despite the fluky winds. Striking the valve in the basket with over four hundred pounds of pressure, a clamp snapped over the refueling probe and Jet A fuel shot into his tanks.

His helo had the least fuel due to having the most men aboard, so he was first in line. His Number Two picked up the second refueling basket trailing off the other wing of the Combat King. Thirty seconds and three hundred gallons later and he was breathing much more easily.

"Ah," Nicolai sighed. "It is better than the sex," his thick Russian accent only ever surfaced in this moment or in a bar while picking up women.

"Hey, Nicolai," Nicky the Greek called over the intercom from his crew chief position seated behind Pete. "Do you make love in Russian?"

A question Pete had always been careful to avoid.

"For you, I make special exception." That got a laugh over the system.

Which explained why Pete always kept his mouth shut at this moment.

"The ladies, Nicolai? What about the ladies?" Alfie the portside gunner asked.

"Ah," he sighed happily as he signaled that the other helos had finished their refueling and formed up to either side, "the ladies love the Russian. They don't need to know I grew up in Maryland and I learn my great-great-grandfather's native tongue at the University called Virginia."

He sounded so pleased that Pete wished he'd done the same rather than study Japanese and Mandarin.

Another two hours of—Thank God—straight-and-level flight at altitude through the breaking dawn and they landed on the aircraft carrier awaiting them in the Bay of Bengal. India had agreed to turn a blind eye as long as the Americans never actually touched their soil.

Once standing on the deck—and the worst of the kinks had been worked out—he pulled his team together: six pilots and seven crew chiefs.

"Honor to serve!" He saluted them sharply.

"Hell yeah!" They shouted in unison and saluted in turn. It was their version of spiking the football in the end zone.

A petty officer in a bright green vest appeared at his elbow, "Follow me please, sir." He pointed toward the Navy-gray command structure that towered above the carrier's deck. The rear admiral of the entire carrier strike group was waiting for him just outside the entrance. Not a good idea to keep a one-star waiting, so he waved at the team.

"See you in the mess for dinner," he shouted to the crew over the noise of an F-18 Hornet fighter jet trapping on the #2 wire. After two days of surviving on MREs while squatting on the Tibetan tundra, he was ready for a steak, a burger, a mountain of pasta, whatever. Or maybe all three.

The green escorted him across the hazards of the busy flight deck. Pete had kept his helmet on to buffer the noise, but even at that he winced as another Hornet fired up and was flung aloft by the catapult.

"Orders, Major Napier," the Rear Admiral handed him a folded sheet the moment he arrived. "Hate to lose you." He saluted, which Pete automatically returned before looking down at the sheet of paper in his hands. The man was gone before the import of Pete's orders slammed in.

A different green-clad deckhand showed up with Pete's duffle bag and began guiding him toward a loading C-2

Greyhound twin-prop airplane. It was parked Number Two for the launch catapult, close behind the raised jet-blast deflector.

His crew, being led across in the opposite direction to return to the berthing decks below, looked at him aghast.

"Stateside," was all he managed to gasp out as they passed.

A stream of foul cursing followed him from behind. Their crew was tight. Why the hell was Command breaking it up?

And what in the name of fuck-all had he done to deserve this?

He glanced at the orders again as he stumbled up the Greyhound's rear ramp and crash landed into a seat.

Training rookies?

It was worse than a demotion.

This was punishment.

———

Keep reading the first book of the Night Stalkers 5E.
Available at fine retailers everywhere.
Target of the Heart

ABOUT THE AUTHOR

USA Today and Amazon #1 Bestseller M. L. "Matt" Buchman started writing on a flight south from Japan to ride his bicycle across the Australian Outback. Just part of a solo around-the-world trip that ultimately launched his writing career.

From the very beginning, his powerful female heroines insisted on putting character first, *then* a great adventure. He's since written over 60 action-adventure thrillers and military romantic suspense novels. And just for the fun of it: 100 short stories, and a fast-growing pile of read-by-author audiobooks.

Booklist says: "3X Top 10 of the Year." PW says: "Tom Clancy fans open to a strong female lead will clamor for more." His fans say: "I want more now...of everything." That his characters are even more insistent than his fans is a hoot.

As a 30-year project manager with a geophysics degree who has designed and built houses, flown and jumped out of planes, and solo-sailed a 50' ketch, he is awed by what is possible. More at: www.mlbuchman.com.

Other works by M. L. Buchman: *(* - also in audio)*

Action-Adventure Thrillers

Dead Chef
One Chef!
Two Chef!

Miranda Chase
Drone*
Thunderbolt*
Condor*
Ghostrider*
Raider*
Chinook*
Havoc*
White Top*

Romantic Suspense

Delta Force
Target Engaged*
Heart Strike*
Wild Justice*
Midnight Trust*

Firehawks
MAIN FLIGHT
Pure Heat
Full Blaze
Hot Point*
Flash of Fire*
Wild Fire
SMOKEJUMPERS
Wildfire at Dawn*
Wildfire at Larch Creek*
Wildfire on the Skagit*

The Night Stalkers
MAIN FLIGHT
The Night Is Mine
I Own the Dawn
Wait Until Dark
Take Over at Midnight

Light Up the Night
Bring On the Dusk
By Break of Day
AND THE NAVY
Christmas at Steel Beach
Christmas at Peleliu Cove
WHITE HOUSE HOLIDAY
Daniel's Christmas*
Frank's Independence Day*
Peter's Christmas*
Zachary's Christmas*
Roy's Independence Day*
Damien's Christmas*
5E
Target of the Heart
Target Lock on Love
Target of Mine
Target of One's Own

Shadow Force: Psi
At the Slightest Sound*
At the Quietest Word*
At the Merest Glance*
At the Clearest Sensation*

White House Protection Force
Off the Leash*
On Your Mark*
In the Weeds*

Contemporary Romance

Eagle Cove
Return to Eagle Cove
Recipe for Eagle Cove
Longing for Eagle Cove
Keepsake for Eagle Cove

Henderson's Ranch
Nathan's Big Sky*
Big Sky, Loyal Heart*
Big Sky Dog Whisperer*

Other works by M. L. Buchman:

Contemporary Romance (cont)

Love Abroad
Heart of the Cotswolds: England
Path of Love: Cinque Terre, Italy

Where Dreams
Where Dreams are Born
Where Dreams Reside
Where Dreams Are of Christmas*
Where Dreams Unfold
Where Dreams Are Written

Science Fiction / Fantasy

Deities Anonymous
Cookbook from Hell: Reheated
Saviors 101

Single Titles
The Nara Reaction
Monk's Maze
the Me and Elsie Chronicles

Non-Fiction

Strategies for Success
Managing Your Inner Artist/Writer
Estate Planning for Authors*
Character Voice
Narrate and Record Your Own Audiobook*

Short Story Series by M. L. Buchman:

Romantic Suspense

Delta Force
Th Delta Force Shooters
The Delta Force Warriors

Firehawks
The Firehawks Lookouts
The Firehawks Hotshots
The Firebirds

The Night Stalkers
The Night Stalkers 5D Stories
The Night Stalkers 5E Stories
The Night Stalkers CSAR
The Night Stalkers Wedding Stories

US Coast Guard

White House Protection Force

Contemporary Romance

Eagle Cove

Henderson's Ranch*

Where Dreams

Action-Adventure Thrillers

Dead Chef

Miranda Chase Origin Stories

Science Fiction / Fantasy

Deities Anonymous

Other
The Future Night Stalkers
Single Titles

SIGN UP FOR M. L. BUCHMAN'S NEWSLETTER TODAY

and receive:
Release News
Free Short Stories
a Free Book

Get your free book today. Do it now.
free-book.mlbuchman.com

www.ingramcontent.com/pod-product-compliance
Lightning Source LLC
Chambersburg PA
CBHW030639130626
46552CB00002B/923